For more than forty years,
Yearling has been the leading name
in classic and award-winning literature
for young readers.

Yearling books feature children's
favorite authors and characters,
providing dynamic stories of adventure,
humor, history, mystery, and fantasy.

Trust Yearling paperbacks to entertain,
inspire, and promote the love of reading
in all children.

THE FUTURE
IS NOW!

Read all the Time Surfers books:

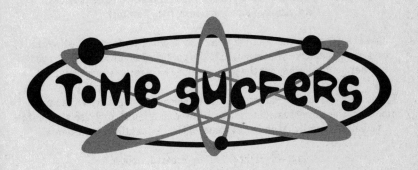

SHOCK WAVE

ILLUSTRATED BY KIM MULKEY

A YEARLING BOOK

Published by Yearling, an imprint of Random House Children's Books,
a division of Random House, Inc., New York

This is a work of fiction. Names, characters, places, and incidents either are the
product of the author's imagination or are used fictitiously. Any resemblance to
actual persons, living or dead, events, or locales is entirely coincidental.

Visit us on the Web! www.randomhouse.com/kids

Educators and librarians, for a variety of teaching tools,
visit us at www.randomhouse.com/teachers

ISBN: 978-0-553-48464-9
Printed in the United States of America
Originally published by Bantam Skylark in 1997
First Yearling Edition January 2009
11 10 9 8 7 6 5 4 3 2

For Jane and Lucy,
the stars in my universe

CHAPTER
* 1 *

Sudden light exploded in the distant darkness of space. Incredible speed collided with unmoving rock, creating a shock wave of thundering, jagged, swirling heat.

Then the light and heat collapsed once again into darkness.

And out of the darkness, a shape heaved itself from twisted metal and clumps of greenery and began to crawl. A shape. A thing. A creature.

Almost at once, the creature started to think. And its thoughts were dark. *Is this the beginning of time? Or just the beginning of my time?*

The creature dragged itself through the

twisted vines. It scraped the ground. It spoke. *I shall master this universe. I am Zoa.*

Light glinted through the green depths.

Zoa crawled. *Yes. If I am nothing else, at least I am . . . alive!*

"How do I look?" Ned Banks stood in front of Sheila's Shuttle Shack and slipped on a pair of green sunglasses with little white plastic space shuttles glued to the sides.

"Really cool," his sister, Carrie, said sweetly, glancing over her shoulder as she fingered a stack of T-shirts.

Ned made a face and waited. He didn't have to wait long.

"Really, they're cool. If you, like, lived on Mars or something, Nerd," she finished.

Carrie was a couple of years older than Ned. She thought nothing he did, said, wore, ate, or went near was cool. To Carrie, Ned was always Nerd. That one letter, *r*, made such a difference.

But Ned smiled as he hung the sunglasses back on a rack. After his most recent Time

Surfer mission, in which the evil teenager Kurtz had morphed into his sister and tried to kill him, the real Carrie didn't seem so bad.

What she said didn't matter so much.

And this week it *really* didn't matter. Ned was on vacation. In Florida. To see a shuttle launch!

"The space shuttle *Orbiter* launches in an hour and we've got front-row seats! I can't wait to see it," he said excitedly. "This is history in the making. I can't believe we're actually here."

"Yeah, here. In the AstroMall," added Carrie. "Surrounded by the world's largest parking lot. I mean, hel-lo! It's Florida! We should be at the beach!"

She pointed to their parents, standing nearly motionless at a magazine kiosk.

"One more minute, darling," said Mrs. Banks, leaning over the magazines with Mr. Banks. "I just need a little beach reading."

Ned looked down from the top floor of the giant mall into the maze of escalators crisscrossing the lower four floors. *AstroMall.* He liked the way everything there was named after the space program.

Thousands of people filled more than two hundred stores in the huge space. And just about every store sold space souvenirs. Shuttle-shaped Styrofoam pool floats, space shuttles made of molded sand, shuttle-shaped trays, radios. Everything.

And in the center of the mall, glass elevators took shoppers from one floor to another. A large fountain blossomed at the bottom.

"I wonder if we'll be able to feel the heat at the launch. Five huge engines sending—"

"Done!" said Mrs. Banks, paying for a copy of *Time* magazine. She stuffed it into her beach bag. "Let's go!"

"Finally! Sun and fun time!" said Carrie, stomping into the stream of shoppers in the main aisle of the mall.

A cold feeling buzzed up Ned's neck. *What was that?* He whirled around quickly. A woman behind him teetered on her high heels. She nearly dropped her shopping bag but didn't. *Good save.*

Then, on Ned's left, two small boys walking behind their father suddenly looked at each other. One pushed the other. "Don't hit me!"

"I didn't touch you!" said the other.

"Strange," Ned said to himself. It was true—the first boy hadn't hit the other one.

Ned's sense of adventure kicked in. His brain tingled the way it always did when he was on a mission.

A Time Surfer mission.

In his many missions as a Time Surfer, Ned had learned to *feel* the future. The present day had a certain feeling about it, and so did the future.

Here, in the AstroMall, he felt the future.

"I'm just going to check out the stores downstairs," he told his parents. "I'll meet you guys at the garage level in a minute!"

"Don't get lost. You'll make us late!" his sister snapped. Then she blinked. "I can't believe I told him, "Don't get lost'! I'm getting soft."

In three steps, Ned was on the down escalator.

Then, there it was, the strangest thing he had ever seen. Moving down ahead of him on the steps was a glittering patch of blurry air.

"Totally weird!" Ned gasped as he watched

the form. It was almost see-through, but without definite shape, except for the . . . reaching.

Ffwtt! Ffwtt! The thing moved like a ghost, streaking off the escalator and down the aisle on the floor below. Like air on a hot day, the way it gets blurry when it rises from a sidewalk. But the air in the mall was cool.

Suddenly the thing was joined by more shapes, blurring by the people like patches of hot air.

"Definitely not normal mall shoppers," Ned thought out loud. He leaped after the streaks.

It was then that he noticed another shape flying through the crowd. But this one was real. It was a girl with long brown hair, wearing a T-shirt and shorts. She was blazing down the center aisle, stealing looks over her shoulder.

"Leave me alone!" she yelled, and bolted off, nearly knocking down a man with a stroller.

"That girl!" Ned cried as he pressed through the crowd. "Those things are after her!"

Those things were *not* from this time.

They were from the future.

And that made this a Time Surfer mission!

The girl shot over to a bank of elevators and jabbed the Down button excitedly, as if she could make the elevator come faster by hitting the button harder. Ned could sense the fear in her eyes. He'd freak out too if those things had been after him.

But why were they after *her*?

"No running!" yelled a security officer, holding his walkie-talkie. "Backup, I need backup!"

"Yes!" Ned gasped as he ran. "Walkie-talkie! I've got to call Roop and Suzi. They'll know what these shapes are!"

Ned spun around a corner full-speed and whipped out his communicator. He pressed the blue button. *Diddle-iddle-eep!*

"Roop, Suzi! Quick, meet me at these coordinates." He punched in some numbers. "It's a Time Surfer mission, guys. Dress to fit in here. You might be around for a while."

His Time Surfer friends, Roop Johnson and Suzi Naguchi, from the year 2099, would definitely know all about these weird shapes.

An elevator came, and the girl leaped in. The door closed before the shapes got to her.

"Nice move!" Ned watched the elevator descend. The shapes instantly changed course and started down to the next level. He leaned over the main railing and scanned the floors below. He'd never make it down there in time. Just then another elevator streaked by on its way down. Ned had a thought. "No way am I going to do that!"

But Ned felt his hands grabbing the railing. "I guess I'm doing it!" He leaped over.

"Hey!" yelled another security officer.

"Sorreeee, sirrrrr—whoooooooa!"

THUMP! Ned sprawled on top of the second glass elevator as it shot down to the garage level. The passengers inside stared up at his smushed face.

Ned smiled down at them, but out of the corner of his eye he saw a dozen or more shapes, moving toward the girl's elevator as it slowed to a stop below. It was only a matter of seconds.

"Uh-oh," Ned grunted. He had to make his move now. He took a deep breath and hurled himself into the air, just as the shapes converged.

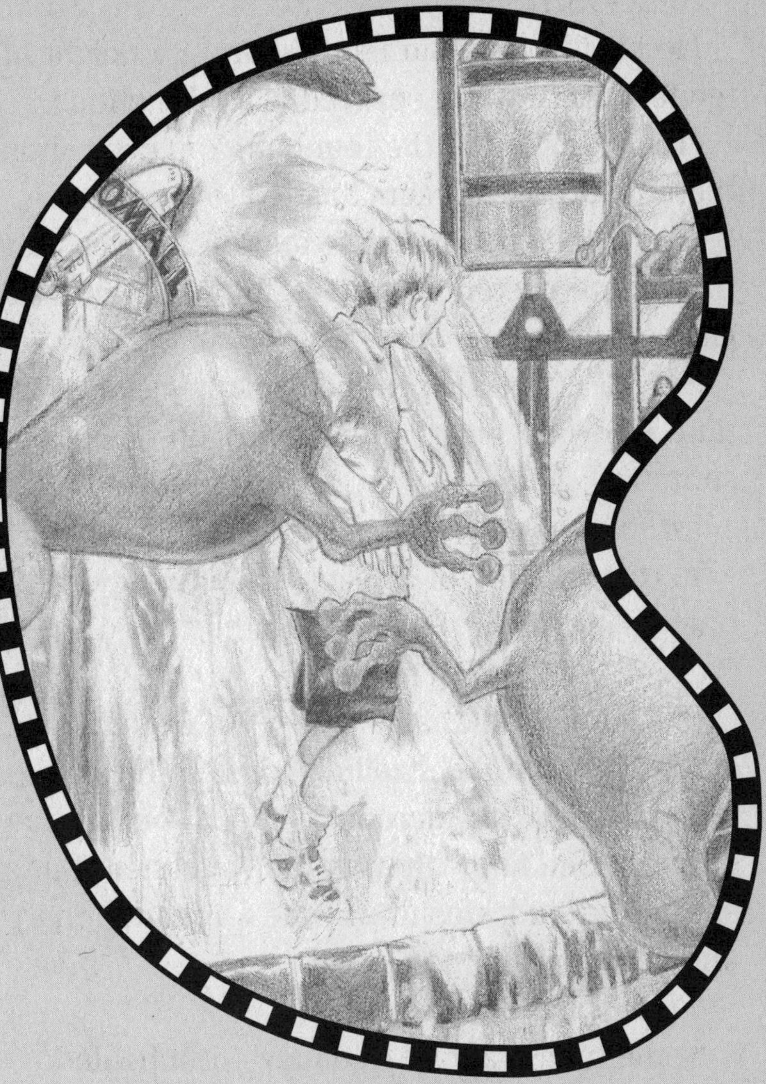

SPLOOSH!

He hit the fountain feetfirst from a height of ten feet. Cool water sprayed in all directions.

"Hey, kid! Out of the fountain! You can't shop there!" Security officers hustled toward him.

Ned leaped up, flicking water off his wet shirt just as the glistening shapes flitted by and the girl's elevator opened.

SPUTTT! The shapes slid back. It was the first time Ned had heard them. They hummed and sputtered, as if they were electric.

"What are you?" Ned gasped. No answer.

In that fraction of a second, the first elevator opened and the girl bolted into the crowd.

"Run!" Ned yelled to her.

She shot a look back at him. An instant later, she was lost in the swelling crowd. The shapes streaked by with incredible speed, but at that moment Ned knew they wouldn't get her. "She's sharp!" he said, sloshing in the fountain. "Sharp enough to be a Time Surf—"

THWACK!

Something grabbed Ned hard from behind.

CHAPTER
✳ 2 ✳

Ned turned to find two big security officers frowning at him. "You've been a very bad boy," one said. "You're supposed to travel *inside* elevators, not on top of them."

"Uh, sorry," said Ned, smiling weakly. "I saw a bargain and wanted to get there first."

The officers tucked their walkie-talkies away and smiled at each other. "Well, can't argue with that," said the second one. "But next time, take the stairs, okay? Now, go on and shop!"

"Yes, sir," Ned said. "It's what I live for!"

The men nodded and walked away. Ned

looked up and saw Carrie and his parents storming down the escalator toward him.

"Uh-oh," Ned mumbled. "This is not going to be pretty." In less than a minute he would have an earful about his bad mall behavior.

Suddenly—*zooosh!*—a shiny blue hole opened near an ATM and two figures skidded out just as the security officers rounded the corner.

"Suzi?" cried Ned. "Roop?"

His two Time Surfer friends pulled Ned behind a public telephone.

"You guys," Ned started, "I saw weird blurry shapes streaking all over the mall and—"

Ned stopped. Suzi was wearing a T-shirt tie-dyed with orange splotches. Her long pants had purple stripes on them and their bottoms flared out over leather sandals. She had lots of colored beads draped around her neck.

Roop wore pretty much the same thing, except that he was wearing more beads. "Peace, Neddo!" He held his fingers in a V shape.

Ned shook his head. "Is it Halloween in 2099? I said you needed to fit in!"

Suzi peered over a pair of round wire-rimmed

glasses with green lenses and frowned at Roop. "You! You told me these clothes would be okay! Look at us! Everybody's staring."

Roop chewed his lip. "Sorry, Sooz. These were the only clothes I could get from the museum. I think 1960s clothes are pretty groovy. I mean, what difference does a few decades make?"

"A lot when you're talking style," said Ned. "And speaking of style, here comes the captain of the style police. Prepare for the worst!"

Carrie was striding toward them, her eyes fixed on Ned with a burning stare. "Nerd! We've been waiting for you, and I—" She stopped when she saw Roop and Suzi. Her jaw dropped. "Where did you get those cool clothes?"

Then she smiled a cruel smile at Ned. "Funky friends or not, Nerd, it's doomsday for you. In one minute Mom and Dad will be here, and—"

ZOOOSH! Just as Ned's parents were coming off the escalator and Carrie was beginning to laugh at the idea of Ned really getting it ... Suzi and Roop yanked him into a shimmering timehole and it closed up behind them.

"You can explain everything to your folks later, Ned," said Suzi. "If what you said is true, we need to get going."

Ned nodded. "Okay, let's shoot over to the shuttle launch. We can talk there. I'll come back to face the music—later."

That was one of the best things about time travel. You could duck out of time, do something else for a while, and then duck back in. All because of incredible things called timeholes.

"Hop in," said Suzi. The purple surfie—the Time Surfer time travel vehicle—hovered a few feet away. The three kids jumped into the seats, shut the cockpit dome, and launched.

VOOOOM! The surfie's twin rear engines fired up and shot the small ship deep into the swirling blue tunnel of the timehole.

"So, what's going on here, Neddo?" asked Roop as he twisted the power stick, sending them into a series of short turns. "You sounded out of breath when you called."

Ned thought about how to describe the weird shapes. "It's going to sound really strange."

"We've been there, Nedman," said Roop,

glancing over the top of his wire-rimmed glasses. "Spill the goods."

Ned swallowed. "Shapes. Moving in the air. Sort of see-through, but blurry. Like if you looked through a kaleidoscope. And they moved really fast after a girl in the mall. A kid, like us. They didn't get her, though. She was cool."

Roop scratched his buzz cut and looked at Suzi. She shrugged. "I don't know," Roop said. "But we should plug you into Brain. He'd be able to tell us what these things are."

Ned frowned. "Plug me into Brain?"

"Actually, B.R.A.I.N.," said Roop. "It stands for Bipolar Reaction and Ionization Node."

Ned gave him a blank look. "Uh-huh . . ."

"Brain is Spider Base's latest ultracomputer," added Suzi. "He can run your description through his superpowerful analyzer."

"Brain is one very zommo dude," said Roop.

Ned nodded. "There's one thing he won't tell us, though. Why the shapes were after a kid in my time."

Suzi powered the surfie's thrusters, and the surfie burst from the timehole a half hour into the future. The small ship lifted over the town to the space shuttle launch site.

"Incredible day!" Ned said. The sun was shining full blast. The Florida palm trees were waving in the warm breeze off the Atlantic Ocean. Small houses were set in rows, many with bright blue pools in their backyards.

The surfie leveled off and began to dip toward the coast. Then Ned saw it.

Cape Canaveral. The Kennedy Space Center. On the distant launchpad a large brown fuel tank rose high between double booster engines. The shuttle was attached like an enormous fly to the three pointed tubes.

"The shuttle *Orbiter*," Ned said softly. "It's incredible to actually be here on its first flight."

"History in the making," said Roop.

"Like your clothes." Ned chuckled.

Suzi laughed and brought the purple ship down unseen on the far edge of the parking lot. "Better stay out of sight," she said. "We don't want to tamper with the fabric of time."

Right, thought Ned. He scanned the spectators for his future self and his family. "Hey, I'm not here! That means that my parents are still at the mall looking for me. I must be in big trouble."

Pfwhoosh! Wisps of smoke and steam told him that the launch was only minutes away. "I'll worry later. I don't want to miss the launch."

They climbed into the stands. Roop and Suzi tried to look casual in their colorful outfits.

"Tourists," said Ned with a little smile for the people who looked in their direction. "From far away."

A speaker near the bleachers crackled. "T-minus one minute and counting."

Excitement rippled through the crowd. Ned glanced down. The front row was roped off for special visitors, but the other rows were filled with kids, parents, and grandparents.

"This is so exciting, Ned!" said Suzi. "The shuttle is one of the very first reusable space—"

"Hey, it's her!" Ned interrupted, pointing at a brown-haired girl in the roped-off section of the stands. She was with an older man and woman. "The girl from the mall! We've got to get to her!"

Ned began jumping down the steps.

"T-minus twenty seconds," said the announcer.

"Ned! Wait!" Roop shouted. "Look at that!"

Ned froze and scanned the launchpad. Steam was billowing from the shuttle and its boosters.

"Shapes!" cried Suzi, pointing.

Ned saw them too. Shapes, like shiny blurs, darting and shifting around the launchpad. "That's what I saw!" he exclaimed.

"T-minus ten and counting."

"Doesn't anyone see them?" Roop started to run down to one of the security men standing by the front row of bleachers.

WHOOOOM! The twin booster engines and the three shuttle jets ignited at six seconds before launch. The launchpad erupted in white smoke and orange flame. The shapes vanished.

"Three—two—one—liftoff!"

The huge engines poured orange-red flames down toward the ground as the rockets slowly lifted away. In seconds the shuttle was free of the pad and heading up into the sky.

Ned's brain tried to take it all in—the launch, the shapes, the girl.

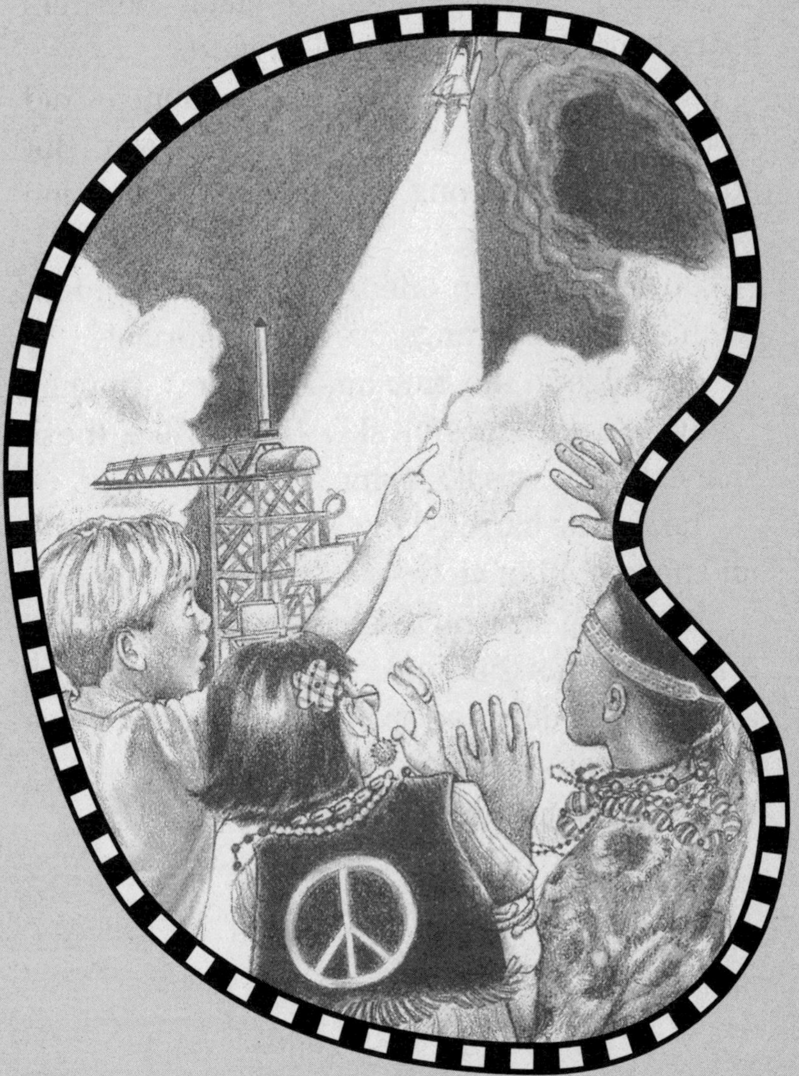

The sky thundered as the giant boosters roared and thrust the shuttle upward.

It seemed like any other shuttle launch. And to the crowd it probably looked that way. But something was wrong. Ned knew it. Roop and Suzi knew it too.

"Up there!" Roop cried. "That dark cloud on the horizon downrange. It's not . . . normal."

A smudge in the blue air. A shadow, rippling oddly in the peaceful sky. Blurry, like those shapes. What was it? A ship?

The shuttle barreled toward the strange cloud and nearly out of view.

"It's being drawn toward that cloud!" Suzi cried. Then, as the shuttle bore downrange, the air suddenly quivered around it. The dark shape moved across the flight path.

And the shuttle was gone.

Vanished.

CHAPTER
3

Ned, still frozen between one step and the next, watched the scene before him and waited for it to undo itself.

It didn't.

"The shuttle! It's . . . gone!" he whispered to Suzi. "It didn't disappear over the horizon. That dark thing moved in and . . . took it!"

"I don't think the other spectators saw it," said Roop, jumping down beside him, out of breath. "Mission Control must know. They must have lost the shuttle on radar."

Suzi nodded. "And I'd bet my life those shapes had something to do with it. Let's get to that girl before anything else happens."

21

"Too late!" said Roop, pointing to the bottom row of bleachers. The girl Ned had seen at the mall and the older couple she was with were being whisked into a white car that had rushed up out of nowhere.

Ned jumped down the bleachers and ran over to a security officer. "Who is that girl?"

The man glanced at the car. "That's Julie Tate. Her father is the scientist Dr. Paul Tate. He's on board the shuttle."

Ned's knees suddenly felt weak. "Where are those guys taking her? Where is she going?"

"To Mission Control with her grandparents. Are you a friend of hers?"

Ned shook his head. "Not really. Just wondering." He walked back to Roop and Suzi.

"Mission Control isn't going to make any sense of the shuttle just disappearing like that," Suzi said. "It defies all the laws of science." She turned to Roop. "Our best bet now is to get back to the future. We have more resources there."

"And regular clothes," Roop added. "Besides,

this is a job for Brain. He'll be on the case in no time."

Seconds later the Time Surfers were in the surfie, sailing out of a shimmering blue timehole and over Mega City in the year 2099.

The future!

"Spider Base, this is Time Surfer Squad One," Suzi said into the screen on the control panel in front of her. "Approaching Landing Bay Five."

"All clear," a voice responded.

The small winged time travel ship shot into the open end of one of the "legs" of the giant Spider Base, Time Surfer headquarters. Suzi pulled up on the controls and landed.

"First stop, I change back into my flight suit!" Roop announced, hopping out and walking over to a set of metal elevator doors.

"Come on, Ned, you have to meet Brain," Suzi added as she and Ned entered another elevator. Moments later they reached the top floor of the base's giant dome.

Striding down the main corridor, Ned got a glimpse of some of the latest research projects.

Roop met them in the hall, dressed now in the standard silver flight suit of the Time Surfers.

"What is all this stuff?" asked Ned, trying to see everything at once. "It's like science fiction!"

"Very funny, Nedmeister," Roop said. "This is science fact. Behold, Robot Central."

Suzi placed her hand on a control panel on the wall. A moment later a wide door whooshed open in front of them. "It's Spider Base's Advanced Research Lab. Brain was built here, along with all sorts of other zommo equipment."

"Like our enhanced Neddies," said Roop, tapping the colorful communicator on his belt.

Ned couldn't help smiling. He had invented that communicator. Way back in the present.

The Surfers passed a glass room. Inside, a robotic arm was inserting a small tube into a silver orb the size of a beach ball.

Roop glanced back at Suzi and Ned. "This is the end of one megascary episode in Time Surfer history. That silver ball is a satellite."

"What's in that tube?" asked Ned.

Suzi breathed deeply as she watched the ball

slip into a round hole at the far end of the room. A hatch closed on it. "Not what. Who."

Ned gasped. "Kurtz! He's in that tube, isn't he? We froze him and now he's in there!"

The whole incident on the Spider Base dome that had ended in the zapping of Kurtz came flooding back to Ned. It had been one of the scariest moments of his life.

"Freeze-dried and miniaturized," said Roop. "A bagel end to a bagel dude!"

Suzi pointed into the chamber. "That satellite will launch Kurtz into a nonorbiting flight path. We can't risk having him land on any planet. He's alive, but he'll never hurt anyone again."

Ned shivered, remembering how Kurtz had nearly destroyed Earth. Kurtz and the deadly species of planet-eating stuff known as the Hokk.

The robotic arm pressed a button on a control pad, and—*KA-WHOOM!*—the silver satellite shot away from the dome and into the sky.

"Case closed," said Roop, continuing with Suzi down between the glass rooms. They stopped at the last one. Inside was a large blue cylinder covered with dials and buttons.

The Surfers entered the room and the machine rolled smoothly over to them.

"Brain, meet Ned," said Roop. "Ned, Brain."

"Hello, Nedmeister!" said the computer.

Ned laughed. "Let me guess who programmed Brain."

"Neddo," said Brain, "sit here and I will scan your cortex for images."

Ned made a face. "Will this hurt?"

Nnnnnn! Brain hummed for a second. "Done!"

"That was it?" asked Ned.

Brain spoke. "The images you saw blurring around in the mall and at the shuttle launch are called Ectoplasmic Constructs, or *plasmicons* for short. They are three-dimensional artificial beings controlled over long distances by their creator. No known weapon can destroy them."

Roop and Suzi looked at each other, then at Ned. "Well, it's not good news," said Roop.

"A time theft never is." Suzi glanced at her

friends. "We have to make sure that shuttle is returned. If we don't, things could change forever."

Ned shook his head. Time travel always weirded him out. If someone changed the past, it would change everything that you knew had happened after that.

Roop paced back and forth in front of Brain. "Okay, the shuttle has been taken somewhere. Find that place and we find the thief and bring him to justice. Time goes back to normal. Everything's zommo again."

"It sounds so easy when you say it," said Ned.

"Ah, but it means I've got to heat up my circuits trying to find exactly where and when—and if—the space shuttle is around," said Brain. "Of course, that's what I'm good at."

Ned took a deep breath. "It's around, all right." He thought about Julie and her father, the scientist who was on board. "That shuttle must have something very special on it."

"I'm going to go change. Be right back." Suzi strode out of the lab. The door shut behind her.

"Julie Tate must be going nuts worrying about

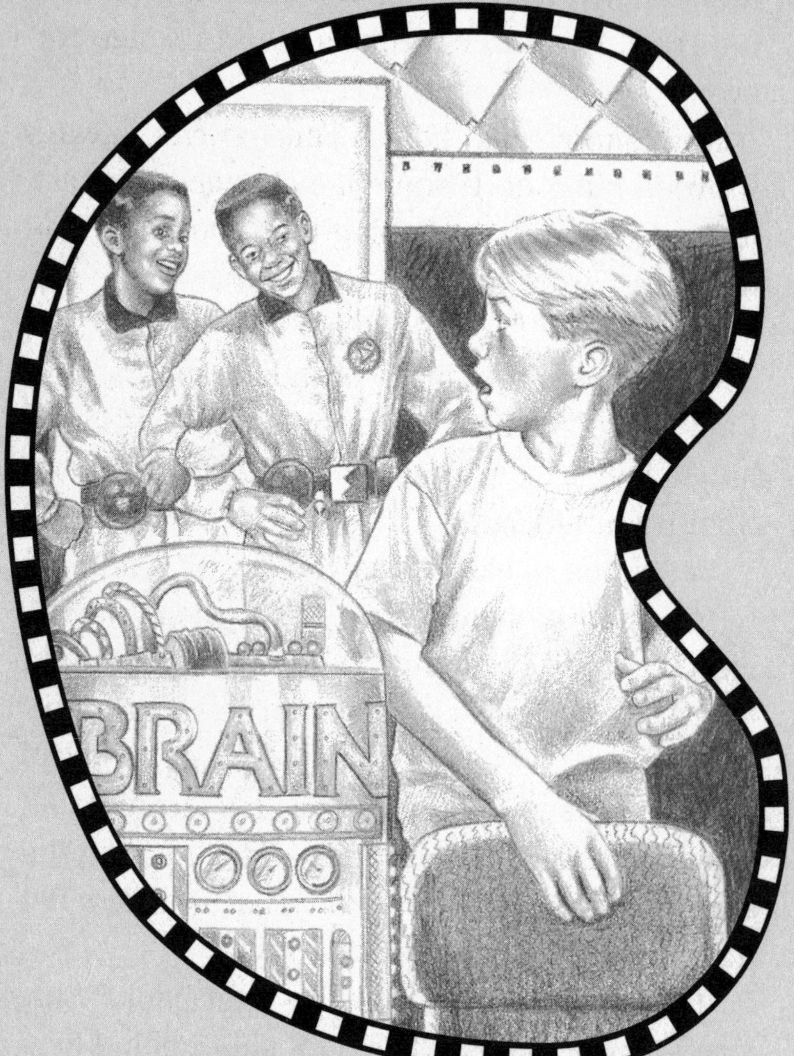
BRAIN

her dad," said Roop. "She might still be in danger herself."

At that moment, the door slid up in front of Roop and Ned, and a figure walked in.

Ned stood up. He stared at Roop, who was standing at his side. Then he looked again at the other person. He stared some more. The figure came forward.

Walking over to them and standing next to Roop—was Roop!

CHAPTER
✻ 4 ✻

Ned dived for the floor and covered his head with his hands. "Watch out! Zonk Zone blast!" His cry echoed through the halls of Spider Base.

"What's the matter, Neddo?" said the second Roop. "Aren't you glad to see me?"

Ned waited for the huge blast. And waited.

He didn't hear a huge blast. He heard chuckles. He looked up. "Uh . . . Roop?"

"Yes?" said one Roop.

"Yes?" said the other Roop.

An instant later, the second Roop began to change. He got shorter. His hair started to grow.

"Oh, no!" cried Ned. "You're morphing!"

In a moment Suzi stood where the second

Roop had just been. "I told you I was going to change," she said, smiling. "Cool, huh? We figured out how Kurtz morphed and developed it a little. We call it Simulated Identity Modulator. Sim, for short."

Suzi held out a small black ball, about the size of a large marble. It had a spot of glowing yellow light on it. The light faded and she popped the ball into her utility belt. "I'm testing it now."

"You get an A-plus from me," said Ned, standing up. "But points off for the scare factor."

Roop laughed. "It's going to be great on a mission. If we can figure out the right way to use it."

Suzi nodded. "It's good if you need a pal to cover for you." She winked. "Like if you're in the future and can't get back on time—"

Blip-blip! Brain's screen lit up.

"Excuse me, my duplicated friends," said Brain, rolling up to them. "My analysis has turned up more plasmicon activity in Florida."

Ned stared at the screen, then glanced at his watch. "It's happening back in my time! Plasmicons are still there!" He turned to Suzi and

Roop. "I should have guessed it! They're still after Julie. We've got to get back there as soon as we can!"

Moments later—*zooosh!*—twin surfies shot back through the blue darkness.

Above a desolate, ruined planet on the other side of the galaxy, a dark vessel moved across the sky. Then it slowed and stopped.

From its smooth disk-shaped hull a beam of light shined. The beam pierced the planet's atmosphere and traveled to the surface beneath.

Nnnnnn! The beam hummed as it moved through layers of jungle overgrowth to an iron structure jutting up from the jungle floor.

A broken remnant of a long-distant battle.

An outpost of the terrible asteroid wars.

Inside that outcropping of riveted iron, Zoa crawled from one side of the dark to the other, scraping the ground beneath her.

Come! Zoa breathed as the beam of light began to fill the room of iron. Her voice was silent.

Her thoughts were transmitted from her mind to other minds directly.

Soon slithering shapes massed before Zoa. The plasmicons filled the giant room.

Bring the prize before me, my legions!

Swiftly the shapes streaked across the darkness, out of the shadows and into the light. The blurry air thickened with the beings.

Zoa called them, her brain pulsing. *Now! Now to begin my work!*

Roop's face appeared on Ned's screen as Ned piloted his yellow surfie back to the present.

"No news from Brain yet about where the shuttle might be," Roop reported. "But he's telling us that he's tracked the plasmicons to a place called the Silver Palms Motel."

"Julie must be there," said Ned. "Send coordinates now. I'll go on ahead!"

"We'll meet you," said Suzi. A second later the screen went dark and the timehole went light as Ned soared through into the present.

"Awesome!" he cried. The ship glided high over a grid of Florida streets.

"Silver Palms Motel, here I come!" A second later the directional coordinates that had been fed into the surfie's navigational computer caused the small ship to dip toward the coast.

Ned spotted a low pink building with a parking lot by the beach. "There it is."

Whoosh! Cutting the thrusters, Ned slid the surfie quietly to a stop behind a Dumpster at the far end of the motel parking lot. He hopped out and moved some garbage cans to hide his ship a little.

It was sunny and hot. Ned glanced at his watch. Almost noon. He was worried.

Some unknown person, or thing, stole the shuttle. But why? What was on it?

And what did this have to do with the girl?

Eeeee! He heard high-pitched humming behind a wooden fence. Instantly he sensed that future thing again. "Plasmicons! Okay, Ned, play it cool and find Julie."

Ned darted up to the fence, his stunner drawn. He held his breath and peered around.

Eeeee! Ned breathed out again. The hum was feedback from a microphone. A moment later a rock band started playing under a clump of palm trees by the pool. Some older people began dancing on the deck nearby. Lots of kids were splashing and playing in the pool.

"See? Time Surfer missions aren't all laser battles and spaceships," said someone behind him.

Ned smiled as he turned, recognizing Roop's voice. Suzi was there too. She pointed to the two-story pink motel. "If Julie's dad is missing, she might be in her room waiting for news."

"I'll check the room. It's up there," said Roop. He headed for a stairway leading up to the balcony that surrounded the second floor.

"Ned," said Suzi, "let's scan for plasmicons in the parking lot. Then check out the pool."

"Good idea." Ned stopped as they reached the parking lot. A breeze was flickering across the hot pavement. Waves of heat floated up from the rows of cars parked in front of the motel.

The heat made the air blurry.

A strange sensation crept up Ned's back. He

35

shivered. Wait, this was Florida. It was supposed to be *hot*.

"There!" he whispered to Suzi, ducking down between two cars and pointing.

A wave of blurry air seemed to dart sideways from a red convertible to a blue minivan.

"Heat goes up," Ned whispered. "That wave is moving along the ground!"

"Good eye, Ned. You're right," said Suzi. "I think we found a plasmicon."

"Correction," Ned said, nodding at the far end of the lot. "We found a bunch of plasmicons!"

At least five blurry shapes slithered through the cars toward the front of the motel.

"Stunners ready," hissed Suzi. "We've got to show them we mean business. Now!"

Suzi and Ned jumped out from between the cars and started blasting at the shapes.

BLAM! ZANG! KA-VONG! Laser shots ricocheted off the pavement.

"Nothing's happening!" cried Ned.

The shapes moved in with incredible speed.

Closer! Closer!

CHAPTER
✳ 5 ✳

ZANG! BLAM! The bright air was filled with crisscrossing laser blasts.

"Our stunners aren't stopping them!" said Suzi.

"Blurry guys heading for the pool!" cried Ned. He chased the shapes behind the fence.

One shape zipped past the rock band and across the deck. The dancers started screaming.

Brang! One of the guitar players in the band suddenly jumped back. "Bogus, man! Somebody's playing my guitar without me!"

Ned jumped after the shape, but it was fast. In a second it had leaped up to the roof of the changing rooms and was skimming along the

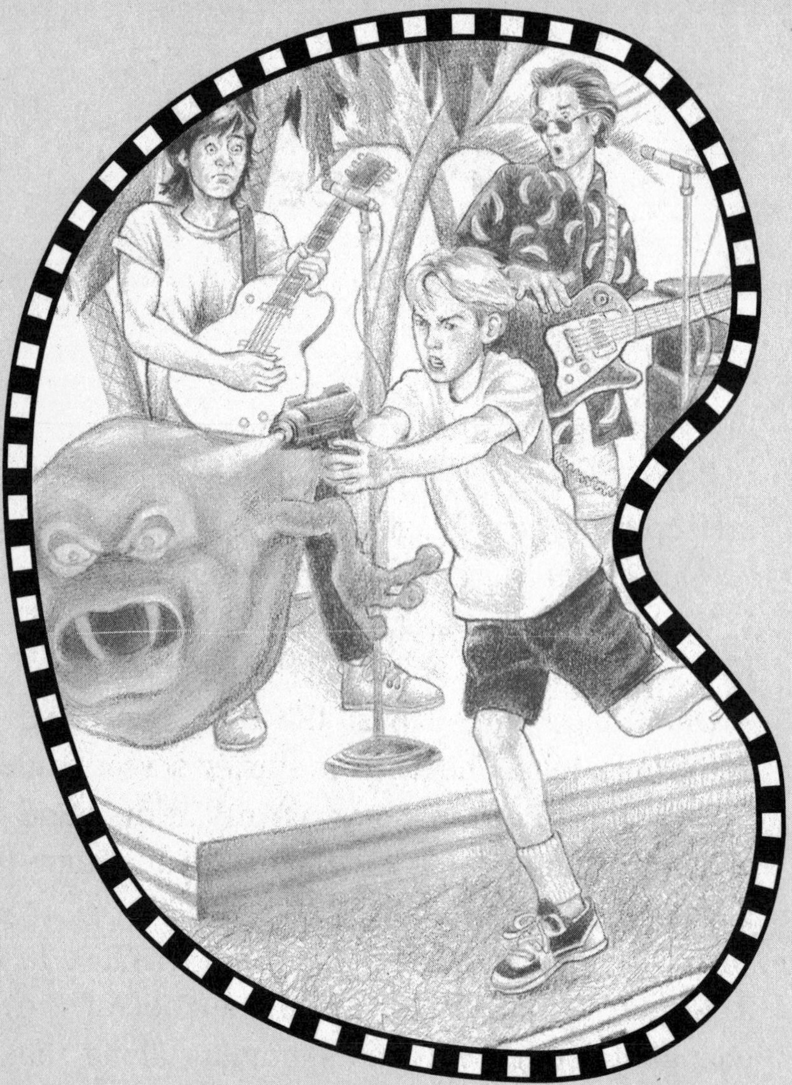

top of the fence, going for the second-floor balcony.

"Stop shoving me!" yelled a teenage boy to the empty space around him.

"Ned, we've got to stop it!" yelled Suzi, leveling laser blasts along the fence top, trying to slow the plasmicon.

BLAM! BLAM!

It didn't work. At the sound of the lasers, Roop charged down the balcony, dropped to his knees, and yanked out his stunner.

"Roop, behind you!" yelled Ned, hurrying for the stairs at the far end of the balcony.

Julie Tate was jumping down two steps at a time, a plasmicon on her heels. "Get away from me, you stupid thing!"

She hit the ground running and zigzagged between the parked cars, then doubled back and headed for the pool area.

"She really is good!" Ned mumbled as he raced along the deck to Julie. Three plasmicons rushed up from behind. He motioned to her to cut into the ice machine room.

Ned wheeled around and shot at the shapes,

then dived into the small room as Suzi and Roop kept up their attack on the others.

"We've got to get you out of here!" Ned said to the girl.

Julie tried to catch her breath. "Who are you?" she asked. "You were at the mall, too."

Ned jumped to the door and peered out. Then he quickly told her who he and his friends were. "The shuttle was stolen," he said. "But we're pretty sure your father's safe. I think that's why these creatures are after you."

"He told me a little about what he's working on," Julie said, poking her head out of the small room. "But it's a secret project."

"Those shapes are working for someone—we don't know who." Ned gulped. "At least not yet. My friends from the future will help us—"

WHAM! WHAM! Suzi and Roop slid in through the open door. "Come on," said Suzi. "We've got to get you to the future!"

"To the f-f-f-f—" Julie started to say.

KKKKKKK! The air turned electric as three plasmicons jetted toward the small room from the deck outside.

"Whoa!" Julie cried out. "I'm not waiting for them to catch me!" She raced out of the room and past the pool. Ned slid out after her, but when he turned to take a shot at the plasmicons, he slipped on the wet deck. "Nooooo!"

WUMP—SPLASH! Ned hit the water.

"Perfect belly flop!" cried Suzi, skittering toward the stairs. Roop followed Julie, rushing into the shadows under the balcony.

Ned's splash hurled a spray of water onto the deck just as one of the plasmicons shot by.

Zzzzzt! The plasmicon darted back, but the splash went everywhere. Suddenly the air exploded at Ned. He twisted in the water to blast the plasmicon, but found himself staring up at an angry guitar player.

"Hey, dude! You blew out my amp!"

"Uh, sorry," said Ned, hoisting himself from the pool. "I gotta run!"

The plasmicon was nowhere to be seen.

BLAM-BLAM! Suzi jumped up to the balcony. Then she swung down and pumped away with her stunner. Julie dashed into a doorway, Roop

41

following her and blasting at a bunch of plasmicons.

"Get out of there! You'll be trapped!" yelled
Ned, sloshing along the deck with his stunner
aimed. "To the surfies! We can make it! Run!"

It was no good. Suzi leaped down next to
Roop and Julie, but the shapes closed in, coming
from everywhere.

In the crossfire, Ned saw Julie run from the
doorway, right into the blurry shapes. "No!" he
cried. Too late.

KKK-ZZZZZT! The air burst into a storm of
electric sparks. Then there was a terrible ripping
sound.

A black gash tore across the air in front of
Ned. He reeled back as if he'd been punched.

A freezing-cold blast of air rushed from the
rip. The plasmicons darted through it with Julie.

The gash sealed up.

Then there was nothing but the gasps and
yells of the motel guests and the sputtering of
electric guitars.

"Julie!" cried Ned.

CHAPTER
✳ 6 ✳

Ned shook his head. "I can't believe we let that happen. We were supposed to save her. Instead, she's gone!"

Roop stepped out from the shadowy doorway, a strange look on his face.

"What is it?" Ned asked. Then he saw *her*. She was standing behind Roop.

"Julie?" Ned backed up a step. "But . . . I just . . . I thought . . . I mean . . . how . . . ?"

"Suzi went instead," said Roop, slipping his stunner back into his belt. "She used the Sim to project Julie's image on herself."

Julie stared wide-eyed. "I can't believe she did that."

"Suzi will have a better chance against the plasmic beings," Roop said, starting back toward the Dumpster.

Diddle-iddle-eep! Ned pulled his communicator off his utility belt. The video screen popped up to show Brain's silver face.

"As predicted, I've located the shuttle!" Brain said. "It's on Planet Wu in the Arkan system." His face faded from the small screen.

"Yes! My dad's okay, I know he is!" Julie gasped. Then she stared at Ned's communicator. "I thought my dad's gadgets were cool. But you guys . . . hey, wait. Planet Wu? I never heard of it!"

Roop stopped next to his surfie. "It's a dead planet on the outer edge of the galaxy. It was discovered in 2052, I think. Anyway, it's been deserted since the asteroid wars."

"Asteroid wars?" Julie raised her eyebrows.

Roop climbed into the cockpit. "The whole Arkan planetary system was nearly destroyed over something called a photon crystal. It was supposed to have time-altering powers."

"Photon crystal," Ned repeated. "Sounds like a fairy tale."

"It's probably only a legend," Roop went on. "Anyway, it all happened before the Time Surfers established peace in the galaxy."

"Peace, until now," said Ned, popping the dome on his own surfie. "It looks like someone is stirring up some very bad vibes."

"But what does the shuttle have to do with it?" said Julie, peering into the surfie cockpits.

"What was your dad's project?" asked Ned.

"Some kind of energy device. It focuses solar power," she said. "I don't know too much."

Ned frowned. "Maybe it creates power. Power somebody seems to want real bad."

"Set flight coordinates for Arkan!" said Roop.

"And don't even think of not inviting me," Julie said, climbing in next to Ned. "If you can time-travel, you can bring me back so my grandparents won't even know I'm gone. My dad's on that shuttle, so I'm part of this mission. Period."

Ned smiled and started his rear thrusters. "Then belt up and let's go!" Roop gunned his engines. They nodded to each other.

VOOOM! The two surfies jetted away from the parking lot of the Silver Palms Motel, up into the noon sky and into a blue opening. A timehole to a far time and place.

Planet Wu of the Arkan system.

After what seemed like hours, Suzi opened her eyes. A bright green light sizzled around her.

And she was moving.

She felt as if she was shooting down a long tube of light. Down, down, down.

An instant later, she stood on some kind of platform, a foot above the floor below. She tried to step down from it.

Zzzzt! A shock of pain went through her.

"Ow!" she cried. Her voice echoed, as if she was in a metal room. She couldn't move more than a fraction of an inch in any direction.

"Okay," she said to herself, "using my amazing Time Surfer powers of deduction, I'd say I'm trapped in some kind of force field."

Ffwtt! Ffwtt! Glimmering shapes flitted around beyond the green light. "And the place is filled with nasty plasmicons."

Suzi still had her stunner, but she couldn't move enough to get to it.

Then she remembered. She had bolted from the motel doorway just as the things moved in. She had felt as if a thousand volts had streamed into her arms and legs—then nothing. Darkness.

"Julie?" said a weak voice.

"Julie?" Suzi mumbled, trying to focus her eyes beyond the green glow. "No, Julie is back at the motel, with Roop and Ned. . . . Wait, who said that?" No answer.

Suzi strained to see out beyond the green light. She was in the middle of a cavernous room. Plasmicons were everywhere. But that wasn't what drew Suzi's gaze.

The space shuttle was there.

The white two-winged craft, with an American flag painted on its side, stood on a platform in the center of the huge room. Its windows were dark. The ship was empty.

Nearby were four other cylinders of light like the one she was held in. A person was trapped in each one. Suzi recognized their white suits as the standard space shuttle flight uniform.

Only one person—a man—seemed to be awake. "Julie?" he whispered.

Suzi was about to ask him if he was Dr. Tate, but she caught herself. "Whoa!" She gasped. "I look like Julie! If that's her father, and I ask who he is, I'll blow the whole thing!"

She glanced down at the black Sim ball attached to her utility belt. "I'm Julie now. I mean, the long hair should have given me a clue."

She could buy some time pretending to be Julie. And maybe find out what was going on.

"Dad?" she said, pretending. "Are you okay?"

Dr. Tate nodded, but he looked tired. "These beings took over our ship," he said, pointing to the plasmicons. "They brought us here."

"Me too," she said. But that was all she could say before she heard a strange sound behind her.

Grrr! Sput-sput. It sounded like an animal. Or a fizzling lightbulb. Or something in pain.

The thing making the noise dragged itself across the floor. Suzi gasped when she saw it.

The head was thick, large and triangular, formed of some kind of hard shell-like material. Two large dark eyes, like black lightbulbs, pulsed as the thing breathed.

S-S-So! My appearance frightens you? The strange voice sputtered inside Suzi's head. The words seemed to burn right into her brain.

You are wondering what I am. The creature paused. *I am a dronth. I am . . . Zoa.*

"A dronth?" Suzi whispered to herself. "Some kind of insectlike organism."

Zoa's body was long and narrow, probably ten feet long altogether. With her ribbed chest plate and thick rear legs, she looked powerful.

Or might have been, once, thought Suzi.

Half of the creature's body was crushed. The rear legs seemed dead beneath her. And at the ends of those legs, blackened pincers dangled lifelessly. She looked like a wounded praying mantis.

The strange penetrating voice spoke again as if to answer Suzi's thoughts. *An accident made me like this. Velocity. Fire. Heat. Pain.*

Zoa stretched her forelegs and pulled the rest of her length up behind them. The way she dragged herself across the floor combined with the sound of her damaged shell scraping over the metal plates sent chills up Suzi's spine.

Dr. Tate spoke from behind the force field. "What do you want with us? With the shuttle?"

Zoa gave out short breaths, like gasps, from somewhere on her damaged, oozing head. *The crystal*, she transmitted. *The photon crystal.*

"Photon crystal?" Suzi repeated. The words brought back a vague memory. "But . . ."

Zoa hoisted herself up on her forelegs. *I need power, the energy of a sun. Then I shall be capable of anything!*

She scraped closer, and her words entered Suzi's brain. *You are here to ensure that your father tells me what I need to know.*

"He won't tell you," Suzi answered.

He will! Because humans have emotions.

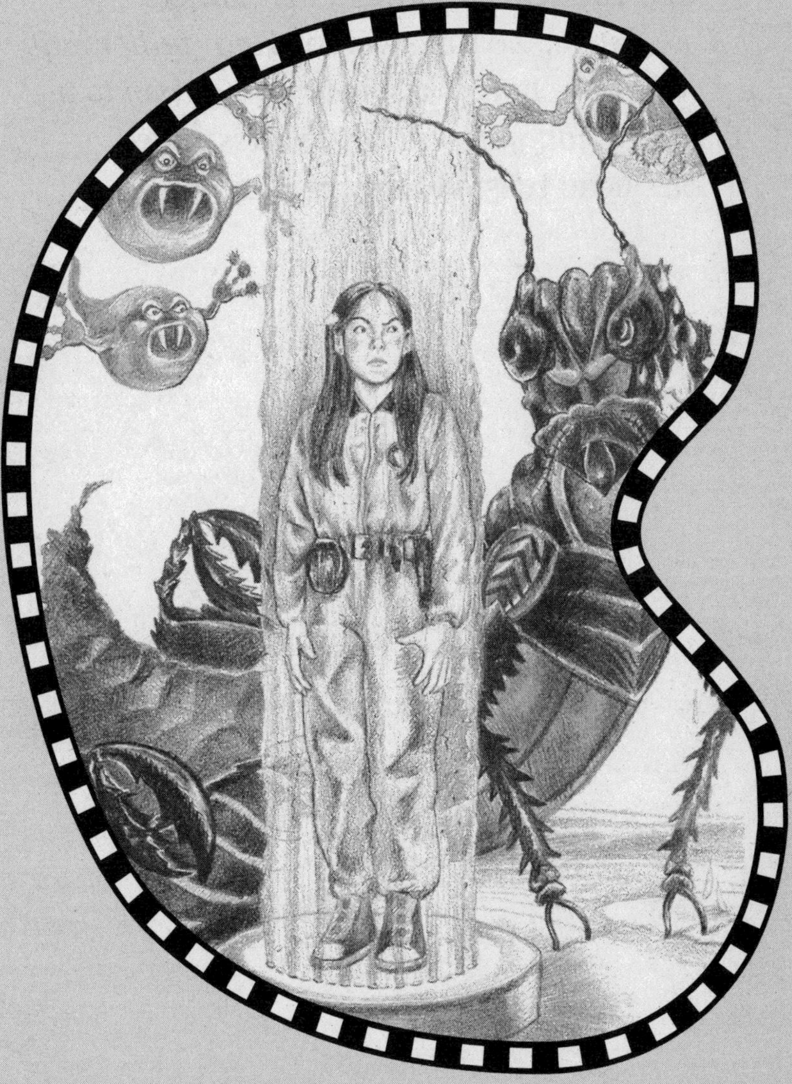

"As if you would know!" Suzi snarled.

I do know, Zoa answered. *Your father will unlock the secrets of his neutronic prism to me. If he does not, you will both be destroyed.*

Zoa's head twisted away in pain.

CHAPTER
* 7 *

"What's this button for?" Julie pressed a small red button on the yellow surfie's control panel.

"No!" cried Ned.

SHOOOM! The small ship veered into an incredibly tricky series of timehole turns. Ned struggled with the power stick to regain control. "You can't do that!" he yelled. "I mean, one degree the wrong way and we could end up face to face with Genghis Khan or man-eating dinosaurs or land in a volcano or drop in at Ford's Theater! It could happen!"

"Sorry," said Julie, making a face. "I didn't think your ship would be so sensitive. I mean, it *is* the future and all."

Ned shot her a frown. "Still . . ."

A minute later the two surfies flumped out of the timehole and found themselves skimming above a canopy of tall jungle trees.

"Planet Wu?" asked Julie, wide-eyed.

Ned nodded as he searched the heavy, layered greenery for signs of life below. "We're on the other side of the galaxy," he told her.

"It's the year 2099," said Roop, his voice coming in clear and strong. He was flying wing to wing with Ned's surfie. "But we don't know too much about Arkan. The asteroid wars left it pretty much bageled to the max."

"Bageled to the max?" Julie looked over at Ned. "I guess the future can be pretty strange for a kid from the present. I mean, the past." She took a deep breath. "Whatever."

"Yeah, it takes getting used to," Ned said with a smile. He snapped on the front hoverjets.

Julie looked at the trees whipping by below them. She was being brave. But Ned knew that finding her father was clearly the main thing on her mind.

"I don't see anything that looks like anything,"

Julie said. "Maybe we should go down on foot?"

Roop nodded from the screen. "Better put on flight suits with oxygen, just in case."

The surfies pulled their fins in and dipped under the forest canopy. Spotting a clearing up ahead, Roop swerved his purple surfie into it and dropped to the ground. Ned followed him.

Ned and Julie pulled flight suits over their regular clothes. The moment they hopped out to the jungle floor, Ned felt a sense of danger. Of fear.

Maybe it was the jungle; maybe it was the fact that Julie's father, the shuttle crew, and Suzi had been kidnapped. Whatever it was, Ned felt as if anything could happen.

He leaned back into the cockpit and pulled out an extra laser stunner. He gave it to Julie. "When you see a plasmicon, just pull this trigger."

"Thanks, I've seen *Star Wars*." She squinted along the stunner's barrel. "But these didn't do much against them at the motel."

Ned shrugged. "It probably just itches them, but it's better than nothing."

"Right," added Roop, checking his weapon's power supply. "Plasmicons are pretty new enemies. Even in 2099."

Julie slung the stunner on her utility belt. "Whoa, what's that?" She pointed to a dark blur floating in the sky above them.

Ned pulled a uniscope from his belt and focused. He tensed. "It's them. The plasmicons' ship. That must be what we saw at the launch site. I guess we're on the right planet."

EEEEE! A narrow green beam broke suddenly from the ship and pierced the jungle nearby. The sharp light disappeared behind the trees.

"Well, they're up to something!" said Roop.

"The beam came down just over that rise!" said Julie, pulling the stunner back out of her belt. "That's got to be where my father is! Let's go!" She took off through the trees.

"Wait up!" Ned called out, running after her with Roop. As they crept over the rise, they saw it. A giant iron fortress, its rusted walls arching up from a clearing in the jungle floor.

Roop crouched behind a tree trunk. "The beam came down there."

"What is this place, anyway?" asked Julie, turning to the boys.

The fortress's rusty surface was covered with rivets and bolts securing giant armor plates.

Roop chewed his lip. "A defense bunker built during the asteroid wars. That's my guess."

Suddenly—*VRRRR!* One of the armor plates moved. Instantly the jungle was alive with shapes, pouring through the opening in the bunker.

"Uh-oh! Plasmo-guys!" hissed Roop. "Dive!"

The plasmicons whipped away through the trees. The panel in the wall hung open.

"Quick, while we've still got a chance!" said Roop. The three kids ran to the giant panel.

Ned peeked in. Inside was a long steely corridor. At the end of it he could see a large white wing and three blackened rocket cones.

"It's the shuttle!" cried Julie, peering over his shoulder. "My dad's in here!"

"Suzi, too!" said Ned. "Let's go. But be careful."

The three kids jumped inside, stunners drawn. The deeper they went, the more they could see of the space shuttle. It sat on a platform in the center of a large, peaked room.

The double doors of the shuttle's cargo bay were open. The shuttle's fifty-foot mechanical arm was hoisting a piece of equipment from the bay. It lowered the equipment into the giant room.

"That's my dad's invention!" Julie whispered.

Ned tapped her shoulder and pointed to the cylinders of green light. Inside were Suzi, looking like Julie, and a man who Ned guessed was Dr. Tate. Behind them were three other light cylinders with the shuttle crew members.

"My dad! We've got to get over there now!"

"Be cool, Julie," said Roop, scanning the room. "We don't know who else is lurking around."

Sputtt! Something buzzed down the corridor behind them. "Plasmicons!" Ned cried. "And they're not lurking—they're attacking!"

Dozens of glimmering shapes flashed out of the jungle and back into the bunker.

The three kids opened fire.

BLAM-BLAM! A flurry of yellow flames erupted from the kids' stunners. The plasmicons took the hits, staggered a little, then charged again, forcing the Surfers back toward the main room.

Julie ran, but stumbled right under the shuttle's mechanical arm. Its massive clamp jerked down and grabbed her, lifting her into the cargo bay.

"Help!" she cried out, struggling to free herself.

It was no use. In a flash the cargo doors closed.

Eeeeee! A bright green light flooded the platform where the shuttle sat. Ned knew the shuttle was going to be beamed up. He had only one chance to help Julie. "I'm going!" he yelled.

"Later, dude! And that's a promise!" Roop called back from his position, continuing to blast the plasmicon horde. But as he said this—*shoom!*—a panel slid down, trapping Roop in the corridor with the attacking plasmicons.

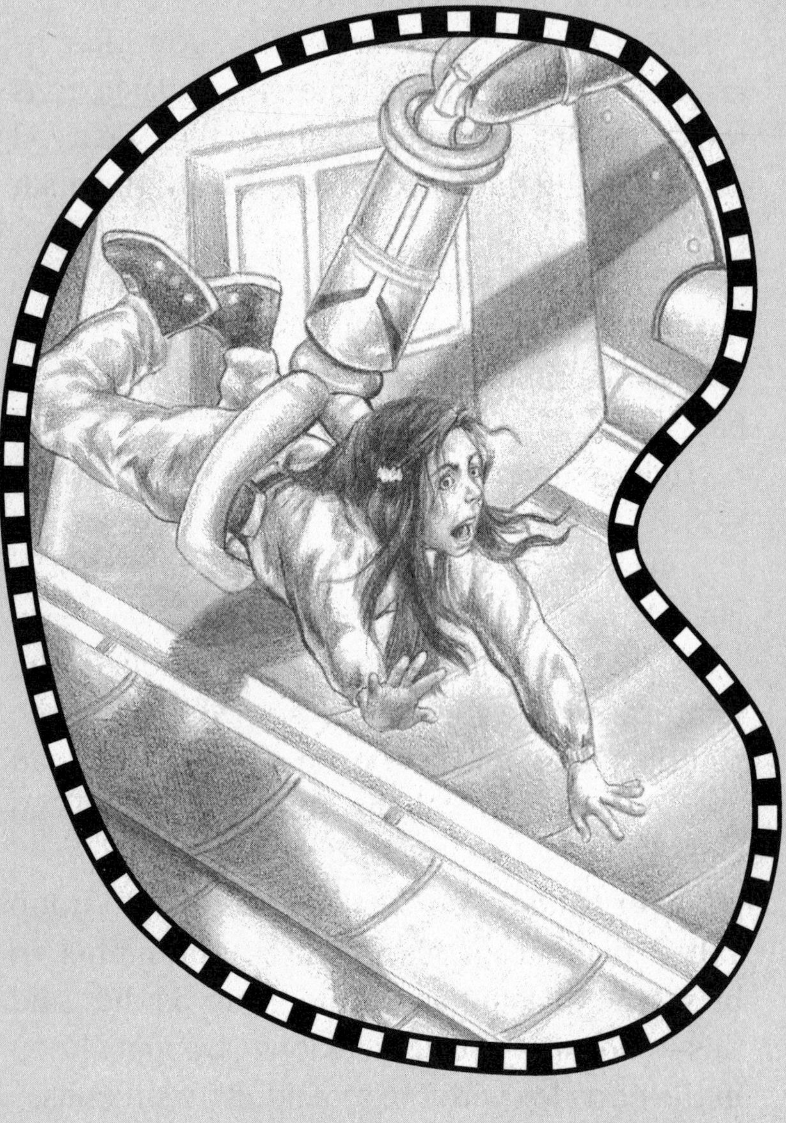

"Roooop!" cried Ned. But it was too late to help his friend. Ned ran to the platform, leaped up, and grabbed on to the shuttle's landing gear.

Eeeeee! Slowly the shuttle was drawn up through the opening roof of the bunker, over the trees, and into the sky. In seconds the shuttle was nearing the plasmicons' giant dark ship.

Struggling to hold on to the landing gear, Ned saw a hatch opening on the disk-shaped vessel. "Uh-oh," he gasped. "We're . . . docking!"

At the same time, one of the airlocks on the shuttle opened, and a glistening plasmicon appeared.

"Uh-oh," repeated Ned, scrambling for his stunner. But the plasmicon was swift. It slid across the hull toward Ned.

Thwoop! Suddenly Ned's oxygen tube fell open, as if it had been slit across.

"Wait! No!" Ned screamed. He let go of the landing gear and tried to reconnect the tube.

Before he knew it, he was drifting away from the shuttle.

VRRRT! A giant hatch opened on the plasmicons' ship and closed around the shuttle.

Ned drifted farther away.

Julie was trapped inside. Roop was fighting the laser battle of his life down below. Suzi was trapped in a force field.

And here was Ned. Drifting off into the darkness of empty space.

So. This was how it would end.

Ned Banks. Time Surfer. Kid.

Helpless. Cold. Alone. Dead.

CHAPTER
✳ 8 ✳

KLANG!

Suzi watched in horror as the panel slid down in front of Roop, muffling the sound of his laser blasts.

He will never escape! Zoa's voice pierced Suzi's brain. *Just as I never escaped. He will suffer, as I have suffered.*

Zoa's chest heaved, the plates rippling as if in pain. But Suzi's Time Surfer instincts told her to be on guard. She didn't know enough to be sure of anything.

"What do you want with the neutronic prism?"asked Suzi, the simulator still making her look like Julie. "What evil are you planning?"

Zoa transmitted no response.

Dr. Tate shook his head. "It's not a weapon. It's a power source. It's meant to enrich lives, not destroy them."

The creature's pod head twisted and her large bulblike eyes pulsed and flashed.

Instantly a bunch of blurry plasmicon shapes poured into the room. They brought Dr. Tate's device over to Zoa.

The neutronic prism was a three-foot-tall, gray, cone-shaped chunk of steel.

The Talaks . . . , Zoa transmitted. *The Talaks want the photon crystal for themselves. Find it, and use it. But I will find it first.*

Talaks? thought Suzi. As the photon crystal had earlier, the name jarred some long-forgotten memory in her brain.

"What does this have to do with my prism?" Dr. Tate pleaded.

Coupled with the photon crystal, your prism will have undreamed-of powers. Powers I will need.

Dr. Tate shook his head. "This is nonsense! The prism stores solar energy, that's all. I don't understand a word of this."

Suzi wasn't so sure it was nonsense. She'd have to see what Brain thought about it later. If there was a later.

As the sounds of Roop's laser battle died down, Zoa's voice gurgled a little.

"Are you laughing?" snarled Suzi.

I can read the future, Zoa transmitted. *My brain probe of Dr. Tate will be successful. The prism will reveal its secrets to me. Zoa shall rule.*

"Don't count on it," said Suzi. She turned to Dr. Tate. "Don't say anything. This creature wants to build some kind of terrible weapon."

You'll tell me what I need to know. Zoa groaned. *The prism's power will be mine. I shall locate the photon crystal. And with the crystal, I shall finally have time.*

"Time for what?" Dr. Tate growled at Zoa.

Zoa twisted her wounded head. *You don't understand. I shall* have *time! I shall* own *time!*

Time shall be . . . mine! And the dronth race shall rule again.

The creature climbed up onto her forelegs and focused her eyes on Dr. Tate's. The black orbs flashed again.

Rrrrr! An invisible beam shot from Zoa into Dr. Tate. He squirmed as it probed his brain. He tried to struggle free of its force, but couldn't.

Zzzzt! The air between Zoa and Dr. Tate sparked with power. *Tell me what I need to know!* gurgled Zoa. *Or both of you will die!*

"No!" Suzi cried. Her plan to buy some time had crumbled. "Don't tell her anything! I'm not your daughter! Julie is safe!" With that, Suzi flicked a tiny button on her utility belt, and instantly she was herself again. Dr. Tate looked stunned.

But Zoa's laserlike mind probe zeroed in on the doctor's innermost secrets. To the fissures in his brain where the neutronic prism's codes were kept.

Zoa gurgled again. *Humans! So weak. I have found what I need. Now the prism is mine!*

The creature's head twisted away suddenly, and Dr. Tate went limp in his force field.

Zzzzz! The plasmicons came over. *Destroy the earthlings*, Zoa transmitted. *I have no further use for them. I have what I need.*

"Hey! What you need is a punch in the nose!" shouted a familiar voice. "That is—whoa!—if I can even find your nose!"

It was Roop! He jumped from a vent high in the wall and landed with a stunner in each hand. "Time Surfers are good for a few tricks too!"

Zang! Zang! Before Zoa could buzz for more plasmicons, Roop blew away Suzi's force field with two carefully aimed laser blasts. Then he shot away the light coils holding the shuttle crew and Dr. Tate.

"This will even up the sides a little!" Suzi cried. She leaped from her platform, drawing her stunner. "Zoa, your zapping days are over!"

Ffwtt! Ffwtt! The glistening shapes moved in.

"Uh-oh," said Roop, scowling. "Jelly boys at two o'clock! And three o'clock!"

Suzi glanced around behind her. "And at five and nine and eleven—there's an army of them!"

CHAPTER
* 9

Ned had been floating away from the plasmicons' ship for seven minutes.

That left only three minutes of reserve oxygen in his suit.

"It can't end like this!" he cried.

Gasp! It was getting harder to breathe.

It was also getting darker and colder. The icy air of space surrounded him. Soon his reserve air would be gone and the freezing temperatures of space would close in for good.

In anger, he raised his stunner and fired a shot directly at the plasmicons' vessel.

BLAM! The blast hurled him even farther

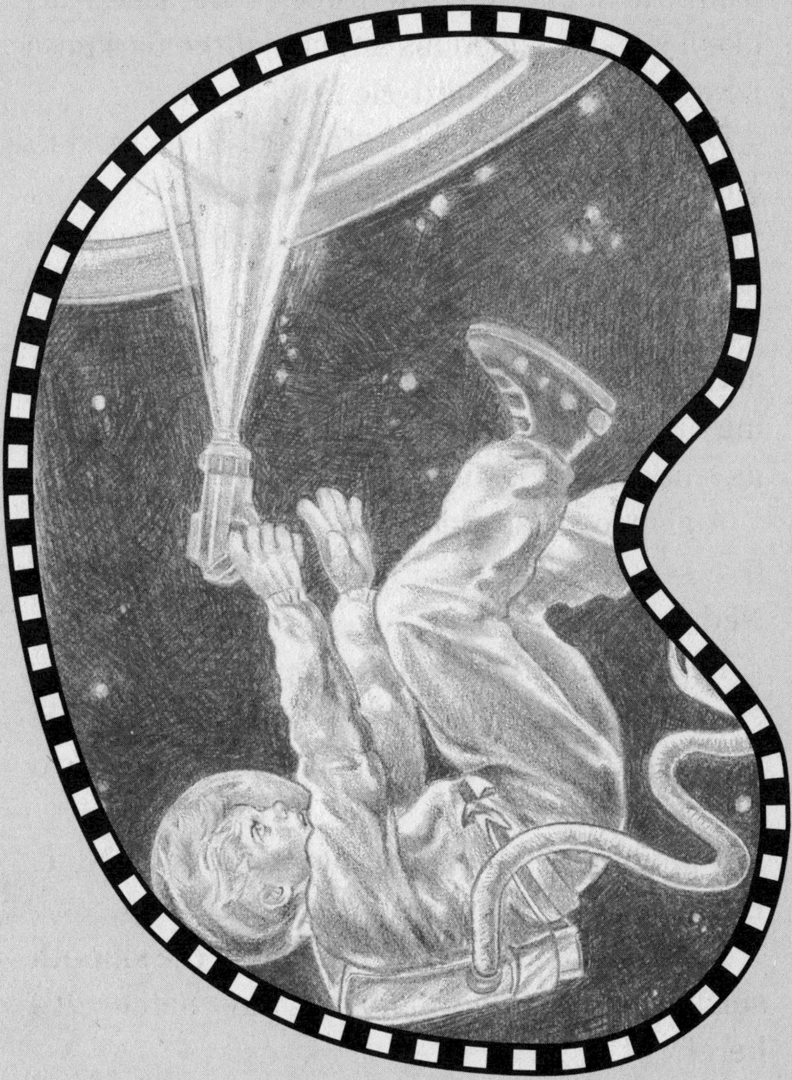

from the ship. "Hey, the force of the laser! It's like a jet!" He aimed his stunner at the darkness he was drifting toward. He fired again.

BLAM! He slowed. He stopped. He started to move back toward the ship.

"I won't die here! There's too much stuff I need to do! I'm not finished yet!"

BLAM-BLAM! Ned squeezed the trigger again and again. One slow minute later, he was nearing the ship. Another minute and he could touch its smooth black surface.

A glance at his watch told him he had thirty-five seconds. Then no more oxygen. No more Ned.

He scrambled across the top of the ship, his empty oxygen tube dragging behind him. He searched frantically for the docking hatch he'd seen earlier.

T-minus ten seconds and counting. Nine. Eight.

Then, there it was, a faint seam in the smooth surface. "Yes! The docking bay hatch! It's here!"

Seven seconds. Six.

Ned set his stunner to maximum, pointed the barrel at the seam, and squeezed the trigger.

KA-WHAM! The hatch door exploded open. Ned slipped through and dived just before the door began to close again.

Two. One. He tumbled to the metal floor.

KLANG! The hatch slammed shut and the ship's internal oxygen supply surrounded him.

"I'm alive!" he gasped, slumping to the floor. He glanced at the gauge on his suit. His oxygen reserve meter read *0.* "Barely."

He fell back on the floor of the small airlock chamber and grabbed the water bottle from his flight belt. "Water," he breathed. He took a sip.

FWISH! The airlock's far hatch opened and a half dozen blurry shapes charged in at him.

"Uh-oh, company!" Ned mumbled. Without thinking, he raised his hand and fired.

With his water bottle. *Splurt!* A low arc of water streaked across the charging plasmicons.

SPPPT! The first two blurry shapes crackled and fizzed, then popped and vanished. The other plasmicons suddenly pulled back.

Ned shot a look at his water bottle, then up at the retreating plasma beings. "Zommo!" he cried. Then he remembered how one of the plasmicons had disappeared when it fell in the motel pool. And the fountain at the mall.

"Water? Yes! Water!" he cried. "Water must short out the plasmic circuitry! Excellent!" As he said this, another wave of plasmicons rushed in at him.

"Thirsty?" Ned yelled at them. "Well, have a drink!" Then he flipped back the top of his water bottle and sloshed it wildly.

SPPPT! The shapes pulled back again, three more crackling and vanishing before him. The rest blurred away down the corridor.

Ned shook the water bottle. "Almost empty. I need to find Julie and refuel."

He looked out. The corridor was empty. Darting down the tunnel, he came to another chamber. Julie was inside, trapped in a cylinder of green light. "Ah, the old force-field trick!"

"Ned! You're here!"

"I almost wasn't," he answered. He dashed up,

found a control pad at the base of the platform, and fired his stunner at it.

Whoom! The circle of light vanished with a flash. Ned held up his bottle and grinned. "Like my state-of-the-art attack weapon?"

Julie jumped down from the platform. "We'll need more than a cool drink to get back to Planet Wu." She raced to the chamber hatch.

"Yeah, a ladder would be good," Ned said, creeping down the corridor. "Or maybe a rope, or a chairlift, or a—"

The two kids peered around the corner. A large white ship sat in the docking bay.

"How about an ultramodern spaceship?" asked Julie. "I mean, what have we got to lose?"

"The shuttle?" Ned gulped. "We could lose a lot. Like our lives, for instance?"

"Well, if that's all, let's go!" Julie broke into a run.

Suddenly—*Ffwtttt!*—the air got hazy as a dozen glistening forms leaped into the docking bay.

"Looks like the blurry boys made up our minds for us!" Ned yelped. "Into the ship!"

In a flash Ned and Julie jumped into the shuttle's pilots' seats. "How are we going to fly this thing?" Ned cried.

"Hey, there's always a first time!" Julie answered as they strapped themselves in.

"Isn't there, like, a Start button or something?" asked Ned, scanning the mass of controls.

"It's probably a little more sophisticated than that," Julie said, looking under her seat. "Maybe an instruction manual?"

"Oh, right. Step one, launch. Step two, land." Ned spotted a tiny green button to the left of his control panel. He turned to Julie. "You don't suppose green means—"

KA-WHOOOOM! White-hot flames burst from the three cone-shaped rocket exhausts at the rear of the shuttle.

Ned and Julie were slammed back into their seats as the shuttle exploded off the platform, burst through the bay doors as if they were paper, and blasted out into the sky.

When he could move, Ned wagged a finger at the button. "That's the one!" he squeaked.

The shuttle dipped toward the planet's surface.

"Just keep doing what you're doing!" Julie said from her seat. "And don't crash, okay?"

"That's my number one priority, believe me," said Ned, pulling up on what he thought might be the throttle.

VOOOOOM! The giant shuttle slid instantly into a violent roll, twisting over and over as it veered into the planet's atmosphere.

"Uh, sorry," said Ned, bumping back and forth in his seat. "Is it too late to take lessons?"

"A little, yeah." Julie pushed the controls back to their first position, and the shuttle righted itself.

"Thanks," said Ned, flashing her a smile. "But we've still got to figure out how to get down there and—"

Then, as the two pilots brought the shuttle in closer, the sky above Zoa's iron fortress turned white.

"Hey, what's going on down there?" cried Julie. "Hurry, Ned! My father!"

"Roop! Suzi!" screamed Ned. "We're coming!"

Suddenly a plume of red flame exploded up from the fortress and filled the sky.

CHAPTER
✳ 10 ✳

WHOOOM!

A fountain of twisted metal burst through the trees and illuminated the sky above the jungle.

Inside the iron fortress, Roop, Suzi, Dr. Tate, and the shuttle crew were blown back by the force of a sudden explosion.

"What's happening?" cried Roop, scrambling up, stunner ready. A squad of plasmicons streaked by him without attacking.

KA-BOOM! A second explosion rocked the fortress. Large metal plates fell from the high walls. A corridor on the far side of the big room glowed yellow with approaching laser blasts.

Talaks! Zoa's voice screamed in their brains. *Talaks are in my fortress!* Her black eyes flared with anger. The plasmicons streaked instantly to defend her.

"We're under attack!" Suzi yelled, helping Dr. Tate and the crew take cover behind a blown-out iron panel.

"Lucky us!" Roop cried. "Anyone we know?"

"Not unless you know things with blue faces!" said Dr. Tate, pointing to the corridor.

A horde of strange, blue-skinned, loping creatures barreled in. They shot at the plasmicons, causing the blurry shapes to spark and vanish.

"I think we got ourselves into the middle of something here!" Suzi yelled from behind the panel.

"Well," answered Roop, creeping along beside her, "we'd better get ourselves out of it! Fast!"

The blue-skinned troops pushed in. They were human in shape, but distorted, with oversize heads and featureless faces.

It seemed as if they wanted only one thing—Zoa.

The plasmicons huddled around the wounded

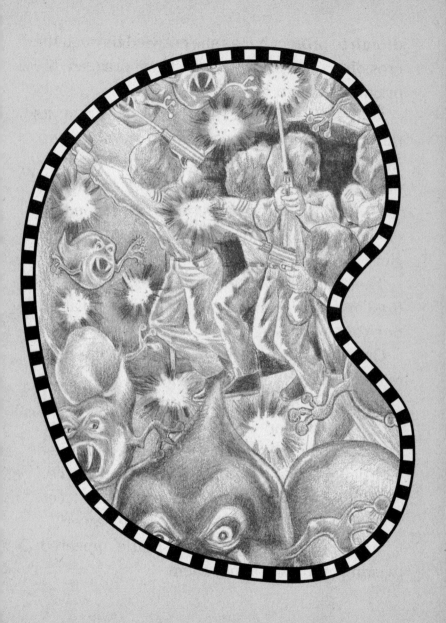

dronth to protect her as she crawled through the crossfire to a side tunnel. They dragged the prism with them.

VOOOM! The fortress thundered from its third blast, more powerful than the first two. Jagged hunks of metal shot across the room.

"Everybody into the jungle! Now!" cried Suzi.

"To the surfies!" Roop cried as he helped the crew out of the fortress and into the thick jungle.

The bunker continued to rumble as the Talaks fired at Zoa's escape tunnel. They paid no attention to the humans.

Outside, Roop, Suzi, Dr. Tate, and the crew reached the surfies and piled inside.

"Come on, Roop!" yelled Suzi. "Let's fly!"

The two Surfers hopped into the pilots' seats and launched the two ships up over the bunker.

"That place is going to blow up big-time!" Roop exclaimed, winging his ship over the trees. "Oh, man, I wish we had a little more power!"

Suddenly the white-winged shuttle appeared, twisting in the sky above them.

Roop shot a look at Suzi. "Either I'm dreaming, or my wish has just come true!"

Dr. Tate stared at the shuttle. "But who—!"

Suzi gasped as the shuttle careened toward them. "Ned and Julie! We're saved! I think."

The Surfers gunned their engines toward the shuttle. The shuttle bay doors opened, and a moment later the surfies were sliding into its huge cargo bay.

"Yahoo!" Roop shouted. "Home free!"

KA—WHOOOOM! Zoa's fortress exploded, rocking the shuttle. The sky turned black. The jungle burst into flames, sending tremendous shock waves far into the upper atmosphere.

Thunder boomed out and over the planet.

"Zommo!" yelped Ned, pulling back on the shuttle's controls as Roop and Dr. Tate entered the flight deck after parking their surfie. "One more evil creature bites the dust. We're home free!"

Dr. Tate rushed up to his daughter and gave her a hug. Julie hugged him back.

Suzi entered the flight deck. "The crew got

zapped pretty good. They'll be okay, but won't be able to help us."

"No prob," said Ned. "We've got it all figured out."

"Reunion later, Dad," said Julie. "We've got a mission to complete first."

Dr. Tate blinked. "But, how can you—? I mean, you two aren't flying this ship, are you? You can't! You can't fly the space shuttle!"

"Shhh!" Julie said. "Ned doesn't know that. Besides, don't you know that in space, kids rule?"

Suddenly—*KA-ZANG! ZANG!* Blasts nipped at the shuttle's tail. Out of dark space came the smooth ship of the plasmicons, its lasers pumping hard.

"They're firing at us!" shouted Roop. "Man, why can't they just leave us alone?"

Ned stretched around in his seat. "Isn't there a rearview mirror or anything?" He gunned the engines, and the shuttle went into a quick roll.

"You sure you know what you're doing?" Dr. Tate cried, gripping his flight seat.

Ned cracked a smile at Julie in the seat next

to him. "Sure! I mean, we've already clocked fifteen whole minutes of flight time on this bird!"

The giant plasmicon ship careened in and shot at the shuttle's tail as Ned and Julie steered into a giant timehole.

VOOOSH! An instant later the shuttle *Orbiter* swooped out of the timehole and soared high over the Florida coast.

It was the exact time Ned had left the mall.

"Beautiful timing, Ned!" gasped Roop. "But aren't we coming in a little fast?"

"Fourteen hundred miles per hour," said Julie.

BLAM! BLAM!

"It's them!" cried Roop. "The plasmicons followed us through the timehole!"

Ned groaned. Then, as the shuttle dipped over the vast blue ocean, he remembered something.

"Whoa! I've got a plan! Hold on!"

Dr. Tate gripped his seat tightly.

Ned and Julie brought the shuttle down low. It skimmed across the surface of the water. The plasmicons' ship followed the shuttle's every move.

"Rear jets, left wing flap—now!" shouted Ned.

Julie gunned the rear thrusters, sending the shuttle into a half spin. The left wing plunged down, catching a big wave.

SPLOOOSH! The plasmicons' ship was splashed right across the front, and the entire crew of plasmicons shorted out at the same moment. The ship exploded into a giant mass of dark energy!

KA-VOOM!

"Talk about shock wave!" said Suzi. "That was one wave that packed a shock!"

"Zommo!" Roop cheered. "Ned and Julie save the world! You guys did it!"

The copilots smiled as they powered the shuttle across the waves and over the coast.

Dr. Tate leaned between the flight seats. "The shuttle needs a very long landing strip."

Ned blinked. "No one could tell me this before?"

Roop looked at Suzi. "Do you think seat belts are going to help much?"

Suzi swallowed.

Ned looked down on the same Florida coast he had seen earlier. Freshly mowed green lawns. Shimmering light blue swimming pools. Palm trees. Shiny cars. It all looked so peaceful.

Peaceful, but not for much longer. The shuttle was descending quickly. In fifty-eight seconds, Ned would have to land a blazing rocket right in the middle of that peaceful scene.

"Suggestions, anyone?" he asked.

Julie turned to him. "Hey, how about the world's biggest parking lot?"

Ned frowned. "The world's biggest—?" Then he began to smile. "The AstroMall!" He glanced out the front windshield. "And there it is!"

A parking lot filled with cars, trucks, minivans, shopping carts, and shoppers was coming up fast.

"Lower landing gear!" cried Julie.

The shuttle roared down toward the ground.

"Oh, I hope this works!" Dr. Tate gasped.

"Watch out for that minivan!" shrieked Roop.

"Shopping cart at ten o'clock!" cried Suzi.

"Picky, picky!" Ned said as he tried to steer the shuttle between the rows of cars.

"Delivery truck!" cried Roop. "Big one!"

"We're not going to make it!" cried Suzi.

Ned stared out the windshield and saw an eighteen-wheel tractor-trailer rumbling about three hundred feet ahead of them. "Out of the way!"

"Hey, what's this?" said Julie, jabbing her finger on a red button under the control panel.

PA-WHOOMF!—WHOOMF!—WHOOMF!

Instantly the shuttle slowed as three enormous parachutes bloomed out of the back, caught the air, and pulled back on the ship.

At the same time Ned found the air brakes.

Errrrrch! The shuttle screeched and slowed to a stop a foot and a half from the delivery truck.

The truck driver blinked at Ned. "Kids flying space shuttles? I must be dreaming!" He shook his head and drove on.

Ned looked over at Julie and squeaked a few words. "That last button was a good button. A very good button. Thank you."

Julie stared ahead, just nodding. "Anytime."

"No, not anytime," said Roop. "I don't think so. Not again. Not for me. Not for a long time!"

FWOOSH! The shuttle's flight doors opened,

and the Time Surfers, Julie, and her father and the shuttle crew staggered over to the top of the stairs.

Waiting for them were thousands of shoppers. Mall security. NASA officials. Fire engines. TV crews. Ned's parents. And his sister, Carrie.

Ned smiled at the huge crowd. He gulped. "Uh, we'd like to thank the U.S. Space Program for its great junior flight training classes. We sure had a lot of fun up there in this very nice spaceship!"

The crowd cheered.

Carrie stormed to the bottom of the stairs. "I've been looking everywhere for you, Nerd!" She squinted at him as he stepped down to the parking lot. "Wait! You did not fly that big thing down here. Uh-uh. No. No way. You didn't. Besides . . . well, you just didn't!"

"Sorry, Carrie," said Ned. "You're just going to have to give me a little space." He looked back at his friends. "Yes, a little space and a little time."

"Time. That sounds very good," said Julie, giving her father a hug when she reached the ground. "How about we all spend some nice quiet time at the beach?"

Ned glanced at his fellow Time Surfers. "The beach sounds good. So does quiet. So does nice!"

"Well, it's about time!" Carrie grumbled under her breath.

The Talaks were gone.

The iron fortress on the distant planet was destroyed. And yet, something gasped with life. In the fire, in the heat, in the destruction, something moved. Something breathed.

Something lived.

Crushed, but not beaten. Broken, but not destroyed. In the depths of the fiery fortress, Zoa the dronth pulsed with life. Power surged through her.

The power of darkness. The power of evil.

She moved through the rubble.

In that place, amid destruction, Zoa spoke.

The future . . . is mine!

DON'T MISS THE
TIME SURFERS'
NEXT ADVENTURE IN

DOOM STAR
BY TONY ABBOTT

Coming soon!
Turn the page for a sneak peek. . . .

Excerpt copyright © 1997 by Robert T. Abbott
Published by Yearling Books
an imprint of Random House Children's Books
a division of Random House, Inc.
New York

Originally published by Bantam Skylark in 1997

Zzzz! Kkk! Jjjjt!

The sizzling fiery ball spat sparks in all directions as it shot through the air after Ned Banks.

He ducked and skittered back across the slick metal floor, struggling to escape.

"Got to get to the stairs!" his best friend, Ernie Somers, yelled out from somewhere above him.

Ned scanned the shimmering steps. "Yes!" Leap up the steps to the next level of this crazy maze of shadows and light. Escape!

But—*kkk! zzzz!*—the ball zoomed to the top of the stairs first, sparking faster than before.

Uh-oh. Things had just gone into hyperdrive.

"Reverse! Reverse!" Ernie cried to his friend.

Yes, that was the only way. Ned had to spin on his heels and jump back to where he'd come from. Do everything in reverse order.

Ned whirled instantly, a blur of movement.

But the floor below was now a swirling dark sea, shooting flashes of electricity like a snake spitting poison.

"The vortex! I'm doomed!" Ned cried out.

WHOOSH! The dark air reached up with powerful fingers and pulled him down. Everything went black. Ned withered. His atoms spun away in a million directions. He searched for Ernie's face, snap-waved, closed his eyes, and faded.

Ned Banks was no more.

"Oops!" said Ernie.

"Oops?" Ned Banks looked over his friend's shoulder at the tiny 3-D figure of himself fading on the gamespace in front of them. "You get me totally zapped, and all you can say is *oops*?"

"It's only my first time," Ernie reminded Ned, setting down his control pad. "I flew into reverse when I saw the vortex. But I ran out of time."

Suzi Naguchi and Roop Johnson, the other members of Time Surfer Squad One, smiled.

"It's just a digital projection of you, Ned," Suzi said.

"I guess," Ned said. "But it still hurts."

The three-dimensional gamespace was set up on a large table in the cafeteria of *Tempus 5*, a mach-speed time freighter cruising to the far-away Omega Sector.

"Holobloogball is truly strange, Ned," Ernie said. "Miniature replicas of you and me, running around this tiny world. And you invented it."

"Tell me about it," Ned replied. "Here we are in the year 2099, playing the three-D miniversion of a game I invented in 2024, when I was grown up, seventy-five years before now, which is about a hundred years in the future from our present!"

Roop laughed and slapped Ned on the shoulder. "Time can bagel your brain, Neddo." Then he stepped over to a row of electron cookers on the galley wall, put several foil-wrapped snacks into one, and hit a switch.

At the same time—*whoosh!* A bulkhead slid up and Commander Naguchi, Suzi's father, entered the galley. He had an array of medals on the shoulders of his flight suit, and greeted the four

Surfers with an official snap wave. "We are entering Quadrant R of Omega Sector."

Ernie tapped a button on the hologame and it collapsed into a small, flat cartridge. He gave it to Ned, who slipped it into his pocket.

"Quadrant R," said Suzi, stepping over to her father. "Where the strange reports came from."

"That's right," the commander said. "In the past few days, three ships have returned to Spider Base with reports of *lost time*."

"Lost time?" Ned repeated.

Roop shook his head. "Really weird, guys. The ships are cruising on their missions, everything's normal, then—*zap!*—it's suddenly two hours later and a bunch of stuff is missing."

Ned chewed his lip. "Missing? Like what?"

"Shield lasers," Suzi said. "And buffer guns and stunners. Mostly defense weapons, but some computers, too, and—"

"Food!" said Roop, talking over his shoulder as he checked the progress of the cooker. "Food disappears from their plates. It vanishes from cupboards and freezers. And when time switches back on again, the whole ship is out of eats!"

"That's rough," Ernie mumbled as the electron cooker whirred. The smell of warm snacks was beginning to fill the room.

"As far as we can determine," Commander Naguchi went on, pacing around the large center table, "some kind of time warp event is occurring in this sector. So far, no one has seen who, or what, is behind it. Our job is to find out. But I must say, it is quite bizarre."

"We'll get to the bottom of it, Dad," Suzi said.

"Right," Roop added. "If time is broken, we'll fix it." He peered into the window of the cooker. "I hope *this* isn't broken. It's going pretty slow."

Ned took a deep breath and pulled his communicator off his utility belt. "That reminds me."

"Oh, yeah," said Ernie, nudging him. "Ned just about blew up my school today. I wasn't sure we were going to make it out alive."

Ned smiled at his friend. It was true. His communicator had bageled them big-time. "It hasn't been right since we got blasted on Planet Wu. It needs to be rewired."

"Ah, Planet Wu!" Roop sighed exaggeratedly. "One of my favorite happy fun places!"

Suzi laughed. "We can fix your Neddy in the tech bay." Communicators were called Neddies after Ned, who had actually invented them.

Ernie made a face. "Planet Wu. Man, I miss one mission and I'm clueless. Fill me in again about your ride on the space shuttle and Zoa, the giant insect who talks into your brain, and blue-faced commandos and weird crystals and—"

KA-SHOOOM! Suddenly the *Tempus 5* rocked violently, as if it had been hit.

"Hey!" yelled Ned, bracing himself against the table. "What's going on?"

Sloop! The bulkhead flashed up and a Time Surfer ran in. She wore the green uniform of the *Tempus 5*'s flight crew. "Commander Naguchi, an unidentified vessel has just pulled out of hyperspace and is—"

KA-SHOOM! The ship rocked again, sending the Time Surfers stumbling to the floor.

"Bagel!" Roop exclaimed. "We're under attack!"

"Alert all battle stations! I'm going to the control deck!" cried Commander Naguchi. "Surfers, get ready to defend our ship!"

Suzi ran for the lockers on one wall and ripped them open. Inside were armored flight suits and high-tech utility belts. She began tossing the belts to the squad. "Whoever it is, they won't get us without a fight!"

Weee-ooop! An alarm whined through the ship as it quaked from another powerful blast.

"Unknown entities on board!" droned a voice over the communication system.

"We're being boarded!" yelled Ernie, grabbing two armored suits from Suzi and tossing one to Ned. "Fill me in later about your last mission. I think we've got a new one!"

KRIPPP! An awful grinding sound came from the forward section of the *Tempus 5*, sending shock waves through the ship.

"Umph!" Roop growled, sprawling headfirst across the table. A bowl of dried banana chips went flying.

Ned fell backward into one of the swivel seats. His communicator careened out across the large room as if he'd thrown it like a baseball. He lunged, trying to catch it before it smashed to the floor.

Suddenly everything began to slow down.

"B-B-B-B-B-But . . . ," Ned started. That was as far as he got. He saw Ernie, Suzi, Roop, and all the others in the galley slow down and hang mid-step in the air. The overhead lights flickered.

A strange hush blanketed the room.

"B-B-B—" Ned's brain seemed to slow down with everything else, but not as much.

Things moved, but incredibly slowly. It was as if time had wound down slower and slower and slower.

Extreme slow motion.

Then, *whoosh!*—the hatch opened with a flash.

And something rushed in.

Something not human.

Worm . . .

That was the word that formed slowly in Ned's brain as the fat wet body with the thick head and small eyes squeezed through the hatch.

And then another squeezed in. And another.

"Grosssss!" Ned wanted to hide, or get out of the way so the things wouldn't slime him. But he was still moving in extreme slow motion, falling ever so slowly.

The wormlike creatures chugged upright along the floor, their bodies curved in an S.

Small clawlike hands at the ends of short stubby arms waved weapons at the Time Surfers.

The worms' weapons reminded Ned of ones

he'd seen in old science fiction books. Tubes and wild nozzles sprang out from the sides. Long silver barrels flared out into wide purple cones.

Clunky was the word Ned thought of.

But he couldn't say it. He couldn't say anything. He tried, but he knew it would take an hour before any sound came out.

Floo! Sloorp! Within moments, about twenty worms had chugged into the room. They yanked open lockers and overturned tables. They grabbed some blasters and some stunners, sniffed them, and tossed them away.

"Find shoot-shoot gun!" one of the creatures blurted out to the others, spraying spit from his big soft mouth as he said it.

Through the spray of dried banana chips that hung in midair, Ned saw Ernie inching his way downward. In a half an hour, he'd hit the floor. Suzi's hand was trying to move. It would be at least twenty minutes before her hand reached her utility belt.

Lost time! Yes, this was it. The worms had done something to slow time. But *they* were still in normal time. Weird. Very weird.

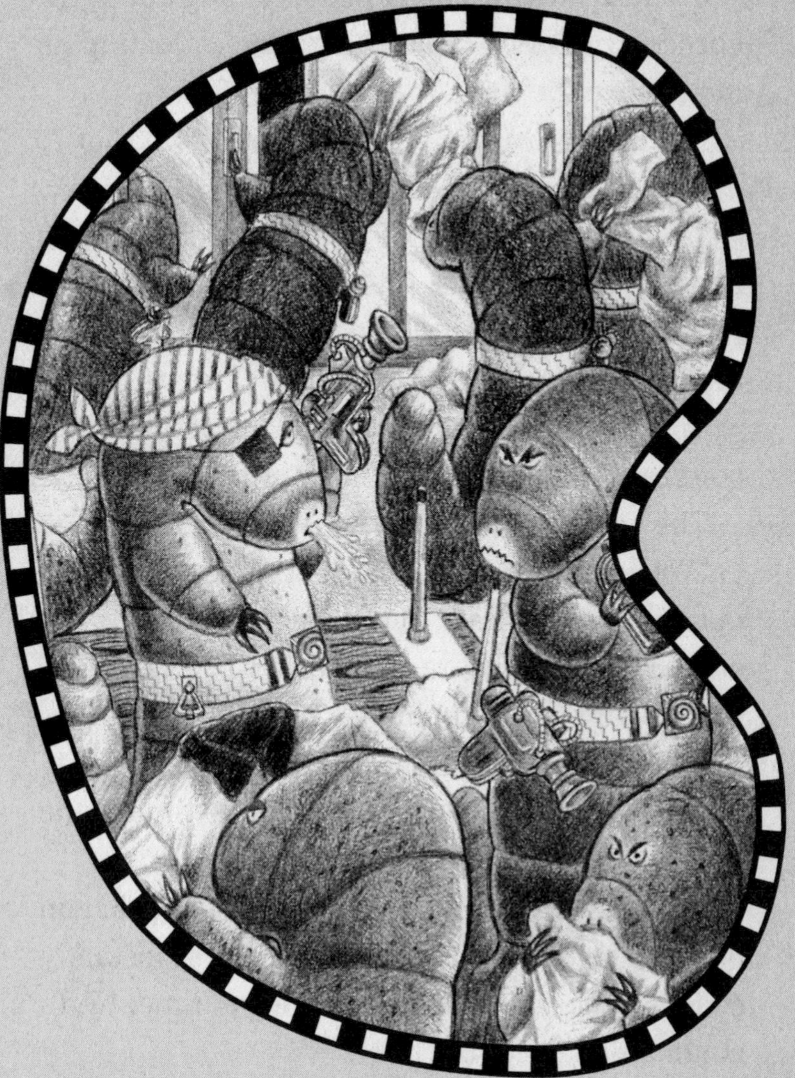

Then Ned caught sight of something out of the corner of his eye. Something black, floating an inch above the floor.

My communicator! he thought. *It's going to hit the floor! It'll probably go off again!*

"Ah!" snorted one of the worms. "Food in cooker! Mmm?"

"Take! Take!" blurted another worm close by, brandishing his clunky gun at the Surfers.

The first worm ripped open the door of the cooker and plunged his stubby arm in.

The cooker was very hot.

"Waaaah! Eoooogh!" the worm cried, yanking out his stubby arm. He jerked back from the cooker—and right into the dried banana chips that floated in the air, inches from his nose.

The chips startled him.

"Blagggh!" the worm squealed. He fired at the chips with his big clunky weapon.

Ka-ploom! The worm's flare-barreled gun burst a fiery spray across the tables, instantly charring the tiny chips. At the same time, Ned's communicator hit the floor.

Skreeeeeeeeeeeee!

KA-VOOM! With a sudden loud explosion, the slowdown shattered and everything started to move at normal speed again.

Wham! Ned hit the table.

Wham! Ernie hit the floor.

"Blaghh! Time . . . back!" blubbered one of the worms, spitting everywhere. He fired his gun.

KA-PLOOM!

"Surfers, hit the dust!" yelled Roop. "Or *be* dust!"

"Ned, Ernie, over here!" cried Suzi. She slid across the floor and leaped with Roop behind an overturned table. Ned scrambled to Ernie and they headed for the table, sliding in back of it.

Two worms trained their guns on the Surfers while the others chugged around the room.

"These creatures are called the Feng," Suzi whispered breathlessly. "They're pirates. They board ships and steal whatever they can."

Ned made a face as he scanned the exits. "They seem sort of dumb."

Roop nodded, keeping low. "They're famous for that. But I never suspected they knew how to tamper with time. Good thing your Neddy cracked the slowdown, Ned, or we'd still be hanging out."

Ernie pulled out his stunner. "It screeched just like it did in school this morning."

"Right," Ned agreed. "Only here it went off the same time as the worm fired his spray gun."

Several of the pirates were tossing food and equipment into huge sacks over their backs.

"Control deck, then go!" one of them barked at the others. "We late! She be mad-mad!"

"She?" Ned repeated. "Mad-mad?"

The creatures squeezed back out of the cafeteria, still waving their clunky guns at the Surfers. An instant later, the Surfers were alone.

"They're heading for the control deck!" cried Suzi, jumping up from behind the table. She looked at Ned and the others. "My dad's up there. We have to help."

"We're on the job!" said Roop.